STUNNING VI

The Demonic Heptagonal Rock

RATAN VINNU

First Published in November 2021

ISBN: 978-93-5472-422-0

BLUEROSE PUBLISHERS
www.bluerosepublishers.com
info@bluerosepublishers.com
+91 8882 898 898

Cover Design:
Archita

Typographic Design:
Namrata Saini

Distributed by: BlueRose, Amazon, Flipkart, Shopclues

This book is dedicated to my parents, for always loving and supporting me and who always picked me up on time and encouraged me to go on every adventure especially this one.

I could never have done this without your faith, support, and constant encouragement. Thank you for teaching me to believe in myself, in God and in my dreams...

Characters

Ratan

I am an author and kind of the hero of this story. I have written this book to just narrate one of my most terrific adventures. This is my first book so please excuse some mistakes!

George

This is George, one of my friends. He likes tasting different flavours of food and is a FOODIE! He spends most of the time reading cookbooks.

James

James is a tech person. He has his interests in mechanical engineering most of the time. And when he makes a special invention, he always tests it on me, and I am always excited too.

Sid

I call Sid a walking, talking, living encyclopaedia. He has vast knowledge of zoology and geography.

Tia & Tina

They are loving twins and have different hobbies. Tina loves music and dance and on the other side, Tia is interested in fashion.

Now you have the brief of the whole team. Let's get into the story…

Contents

Chapter 1

How this story started...

Hi, Hola, hello, Namaste, Marhaba, Salam, okay these are five ways of saying hello in different languages, for more you can refer to my giveaway on the last page where I have mentioned the top fifty ways of saying hello in different languages. First of all, let me introduce myself. I am Ratan, a common man, or you can also call me a common teen to be more precise. I am totally an alien from a different planet, meaning a unique teen in my school with an out of box imagination and problem-solving skills but I am not that good at studies. By the way, who likes the angry history teacher's boring lecture? My hobbies are badminton, partying, gaming and art and much more, but I think it's getting late for the story. OK sorry for a long introduction, I know you can't wait for the story so now I am definitely not here to give a big boastful introduction. In this book I am going to narrate a story about one of my funniest, most thrilling and horrifying, terrifying, mystifying, demonic, spine chilling, back-breaking, bone-crunching, breath taking adventures about the mystery of a demonic rock, so that's too much exaggeration. This story starts with a piece of a silly rock that ruined my summer vacation. Oh! Sorry, no more spoilers here.

So, it all started in a really fun way. Today was my last day of school and tomorrow was supposed to be the start of joy, days of happiness, hours of excitement, time of pleasure and summer vacation; for me, nothing was more pleasant than ice cream in my hand, bright and shiny sunny days and a beach in front of me which would make an ideal summer vacation. I woke up early in the morning, hopped out of bed and stretched my arms full of joy.

On the school bus, my friend had bought mini speakers, and we were enjoying the top 50 songs jukebox on YouTube, and in school, we had a boom-blasting party 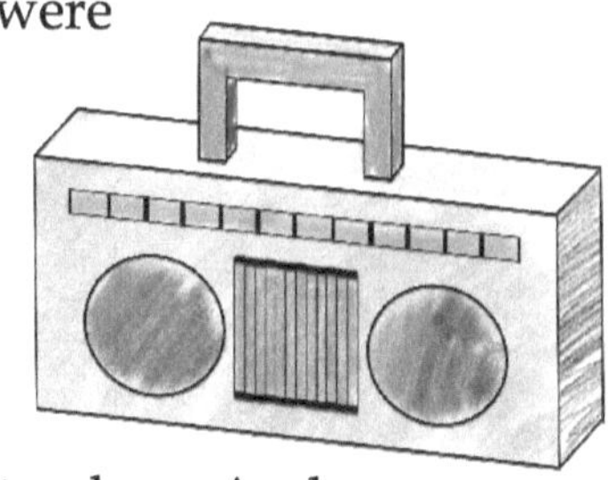 as a gift from our teacher. And my friends, as always, did silly things like freezing mentos in ice cubes and preparing mini bombs to put in a glass of coke and prank others. After reaching home, first I grabbed my calendar, hopped onto my cosy bean bag, got a glass of lemonade, turned on the AC and started planning my vacation. I was lost in beautiful summery dreams, but the future had prepared something else for me.

The next day, a pleasant Sunday morning, the first day of my summer holidays, we all were playing cricket, one of my favourite sports. Our team was winning until the last over struck us, then our scores fell badly. The opponent was playing well, as the batsman was the team captain, and the last ball was a six; our team lost by only 0.2 runs. That's a very sad thing. The empire announced, "Captain Ratan and team Stunning VI are defeated with a difference of 0.2 runs."

You might wonder who uses decimals in cricket but that's our gameplay. The only sad 3 things at that point were that our team lost when it was so close to winning just by 0.2 runs. The second thing was that the ball landed deep into the woods and unluckily I was the fielder and there were so many mosquitoes, and it was a hill. Third thing was that this was the first match of our holidays and we lost it which reduced the confidence of my teammates. After all, it was our mistake; we could have sent James in the last over as he was a good spinner. Anyhow, as I was the fielder, I went to get the ball from the woods.

Chapter 2

Mysterious Twist

I went there with my dog Wolfy, as he was my only trusted partner, he would never even think of leaving me alone. We were searching for twenty minutes and were by then almost exhausted. I decided to go home and buy a new ball but then I couldn't find Wolfy. I went searching almost everywhere. At last, I found a rock with 7 sides. I remember my teacher had taught me that it was called a heptagon. This rock was way too surprising, its sides were made of polished bronze and sided neatly, and there was a glass sphere in the middle of the rock and star-shaped holes all around it. When I saw the white ball, I thought it was my ball. I wondered how it came here. I took my bat and was about to break it but suddenly I saw Wolfy's face, which popped out there. He had purple eyes with blood leaking out of them as if he was crying just like in a breath-taking scene in a horror movie. I was horrified and terrified and started crying, then suddenly an enormous bright flash blinded my eyes. I fainted then and there and no one except me knew about the rock and I didn't know what happened after I fainted.

I found myself in the central hospital when I opened my eyes. I asked my parents, who were sitting beside me, "What all had happened? How am I here?" I was totally confused and feared.

They sadly said, "You were missing for 2 days and were found in the woods by a team of police officers who had ran down to man hunt you after we raised a missing complaint, we were so worried for you. Don't step in that area next time."

I got up, drank a glass of water and calmly explained to them about the rock, the blinding light, Wolfy with bloody purple eyes and etcetera. But no one believed me.

The series of events were unimaginable and hard to understand. After this mess, I had undergone a series of psychological and brain tests, and I got all positive results. No one wanted to stay beside me for some reason except my friends. I went to my friends hoping they would trust me. I explained to them about the mysterious rock and the mystery of Wolfy, but everyone thought it was a bad dream caused by aggressive fear.

That midnight was a disaster to me. I hadn't even imagined my summer holidays would go this worse! Neither I got peaceful sleep, nor my fear went away. That scary night I was even afraid to go to the washroom, but I overcame the fear and went.

Suddenly, I heard noises of people crying, begging, shouting and yelling with fear, "Help us! Help us!" I ran to my bed, hid in my blanket and slept crying with indefinable pain and fear. The next day my parents were not on their bed! I searched for them everywhere: in the kitchen, bathroom, basement, attic and even outside. I burst out in tears. I was completely sure that the silly piece of rock must have done something fishy. Now my blood was boiling. I had no more fear hidden in me. I went to that same spot that day to find Wolfy and my parents. But I couldn't find anyone. Instead, I found a grey bag with 4 things: a book, a case, a paintbrush and a statue.

I thought that these things were somehow related to the rock. That moment, I suddenly decided to head back but a series of strange events happened…

Chapter 3

Into Some Other Fictional World

A black magical portal appeared. I was puzzled and decided to run back, but to my bad luck, I tripped over a banana peel and was forcefully pulled inside the portal. I carried all the things with me, but the book slipped out of my hands. I was completely horrified. The portal was black and a shade of dark purple, suddenly a swarm of dust started circling me round and round, I started to transform into what I was imagining: first I became a pig and then a horse and then the thing I always once wanted to be, a soldier with heavy guns and other war instruments just like the ones in the video game on my PlayStation he actually looks good with a Dragunov and few grenades. I didn't know what was happening. I got a pair of night-vision goggles, a heavy-duty gun, stylish bulletproof clothing, some shining metal boots, a few pocketknives and much other equipment. It was just like a video game character. I felt like I was playing a video game without a controller in virtual reality (VR).

I fell on some island confused and there was a nearby house with no one living inside it. I didn't know what to do. I cooked some cup

 noodles because that was the only thing I knew how to cook. Anyways I am not that good at cooking. Last time, I burnt a fish fry. And then I finally had a bad night's sleep. I hope you know what I mean, I really missed my fluffy pillow, my soft mattress and, last but not the least, my cosy warm blanket in which I would curl up as a baby. It was tremendously difficult to sleep so I was passing the time by daydreaming at night. That midnight, the statue, which I had found in that bag, came out slowly and started glowing. He came nearer and nearer and started talking. I was already frozen due to the cold climate, but now I was ultimately frozen with fear just like an iceberg and my condition was so worse that I couldn't speak anything. I was seeing mythical things like this for the first time. I never believed in ghosts. There was a bright green light glowing around him when he said, "Hey little child, there's absolutely no need to fear me. I am the statue soul, your guardian for this quest. I will tell you the reason for you being called here. You are the chosen one to save this world from the uprising demonic curse. This world is in

danger from the soul of Mighty Ranges. If you don't complete this quest, soon this world will turn into an ugly graveyard."

I stammered "What kind of demonic curse? Why only me? What quest?"

He replied, "A long time ago in the Roman times there used to be a mighty emperor known as Mighty Ranges. He was the king of the seven seas, emperor of seven lands and the owner of the seven precious crystals. He was a calm-minded, good king, and all willingly excepted his paramountcy and wanted him to be the ruler. But one day, in his royal palace, his trustworthy minister passed away and then he got replaced by a wicked minister. The minister misled the king and attracted him to greediness and the dream to take over gods. He got the king into a wicked state, when he committed bad deeds to frighten and rule the gods. One day, the almighty came down from the clouds and the king disrespected him boasting about his superiority over the gods. The almighty took all the crystals and finished the evil king. And now his unpleasant soul has possessed the heptagonal rock. You have to hand him the seven crystals to give him peace."

The statue soul did some magic, and he turned a cricket ball into a globe which had 7 places marked on it, he said, "Collect these 7 crystals and return. Don't worry, I will always be near you for your guidance."

I agreed, as I had to save Wolfy, my family and all the people in danger too. He gave me a special bike for support in the journey. Its speciality lay in its engine; it had dual tech motors and was soundproof, fast and had many other features such as sticky tyres, huge leaps, helicopter flight and more. I thanked the statue soul and asked what everything in this bag was for.

He said, "Whatever is drawn with the magic paintbrush in the air comes to life. The book that you found is about Mighty Ranges and the 7 crystals. And the case is to store the 7 crystals safely; it is fire-resistant, water-resistant, and even breakproof and is made by one of the strongest metals in the universe and is prone to any form of black magic. Last but not least, I, the statue soul, am for your guidance in your quest. All the best, hope you succeed." I thanked him and headed to the hunt for the first crystal…

Chapter 4

A Volcanic Spit

I started to move ahead to get the fire crystal. This quest was completely different from my expectations and way harder than I had ever thought because I was in some fictional world. It took me a very long … long …long… time to reach there. I wouldn't even step in that area in my dream. It was a real-life nightmare. The whole area was covered with a layer of thick smoke. I had to draw an oxygen mask with my magic paintbrush. Thank God that my drawing was great. At least I could take a breath of relief. The whole area was covered with dense smoke which was as thick as a brick wall.

I also drew night vision goggles. The area was filled with lava, smoke and volcanoes that were bursting out every minute as if they wanted to spit on me and I named this phenomenon The Volcanic Spit. In the midpoint of the land of the volcanoes, I saw a tall pillar made of fine quartz and obsidian; it was taller than all volcanoes. I saw something shining on top of it and I thought it to be the fire crystal. At the drop of a hat, I started climbing on it and when I was halfway through suddenly BOOM! Something bashed on me ruthlessly. It was an evil Pegasus, or I think it was a unicorn with a shiny red horn on top.

First of all, I was confused about whether it was a unicorn or a Pegasus, so I named it Pega-corn.

I was a baby ant in front of that Pega-corn. I hid behind a rock but not for long, he crushed the rock with his toes. I ran at the speed of lightning and suddenly I tripped and found myself hanging on the edge of a cliff. The evil Pega-corn walked away but my hand slipped out. I lost hope totally and gave up. My head was about to hit the ground. Suddenly I felt someone lasso me with a rope and pull me up. I thought I was dreaming in the afterlife. I nearly fainted and when I woke up, I saw a few recognizable faces: they were my friends! George, James, Tia, Tina, and Sid. I wondered how my friends could come here. Without them even knowing anything about the incident, they started to narrate a huge story about how they reached here...

George said, "We were worried about you, when you said that terrific story about the mysterious rock, we didn't believe you but our hearts kept haunting us. So, we decided to check it for ourselves."

James continued "We went to that mysterious faint spot of yours to get a clear picture of things." Tina replied "Then we found a statue known as the statue soul. He gave us his guidance and explained the quest to us. So now we're with you."

I said, "So let's go and defeat that evil Pega-corn now. Get your weapons ready!"

We then rapidly started attacking the Pega-corn, but the Pega-corn was magical. He defended himself by a magical barrier surrounding him, and nothing worked against it, not even our magical weapons. We had bruises from head to toe but the Pega-corn was pretty active.

Tia said, "This is impossible. This quest will definitely lead us to the path of heaven. "We should rather quit, there's no way to win, let's leave all this mess and run away and rather live like scavengers in the jungle."

"I got an idea!" I said. "There were two weird things that I noticed about that Pega-corn. First of all, when I was hanging on the cliff the Pega-corn didn't chase me. That means he has a certain limit and can't move further. And the second one is his horn; it was not being covered by his magical barrier so we can consider it as its weakness." After my explanation everyone got some hope and then we followed the same strategy.

Chapter 5

The Fight with the Cursed Pega-corn

"Good idea!" said George. Sid and Tia didn't join, as their legs were badly injured. Tina was aiding Tia and Sid. Our main goal was to somehow remove his horn from his head. James and George were waiting for my signal. I went to the front and started attacking rapidly at his horn. The first few minutes were going well but then he started spiting flames. I rode my bike near his leg and circled him. I trapped him in his own trap and there was fire all around him but then I realized I was trapped too. Then he caught me with his tail. I gave James and George my secret signal and then in a blink of an eye he threw me from his tail, and I was on his head next to his horn.

According to the plan, James and George started attacking to distract the Pega-corn. Both started attacking his tail. I tripped and rolled and was on his back and then suddenly he also injured James and George and after all, he was free of enemies I was the only one left. He was cheerfully celebrating his victory, I guess. I thought today was my last day. Suddenly when he turned back, a bright and bold light broke his horn. The Pega-corn and I both fell . I was safe and sound. After the light cleared, I saw Tina with Laser operated sniper rifle in her hand. I never knew a sniper rifle could be so powerful. But the removal of his horn wasn't his end. That just reduced his size but he was still alive. And now I thought that the only way to finish him was to bring him out of his boundary; he was the size of a horse. I jumped and started controlling him. He was not that easy. Finally, I was successful. He fainted. Tina got the fire crystal.

We then packed up and were leaving together celebrating our victory but just as we were leaving, I saw a bright pink light shining. The Pega-corn was transformed into some other creature. I was shocked so I went nearer, my friends tried to stop me, but I just went near him.

He was speaking to me and said, "Thank you for saving me, my friend. I am very grateful to you. I am actually an unicorn, but I was cursed by an evil king to be an demon like creature. You are a real hero; you have freed me from the curse" Now I understood that he was a unicorn but I would still like to call him Pega-corn.

We then moved ahead to the next destination, the Witch City to get the crystal of psychic. The Witch City was also known as the Witchy Place. Our Pega-corn friend told us that he would accompany us on the journey. He went inside the fire crystal, and we could call him for help whenever we needed him.

Chapter 6

The Witch City

The land of witches was not much far until we had our superbikes given to us by the statue soul. It was just like a highly developed fictional city. The sky was violet in colour with a shade of light pink and there were bats almost everywhere and the whole city was filled with a strong odour. As we were moving ahead, we saw a board that read 'Welcome to Witch City'.

Suddenly, a witch riding a long broomstick with a few pillows came in front of us and she said, "Daerhoman beans wulcome to da sitty of watches." My friends started to control their laughter to not be rude.

I whispered to my friends, "She actually meant 'Dear human beings welcome to the city of witches.' She would fail in even a grade 2 grammar test." Then she said, "Kom sot on mi baroom-stack taxi its fur Fri I wulltukeyuwherevuryuwunt."

My friends burst out in laughter, and I whispered to them again, "This lady is too funny she means 'Come sit on my broomstick-taxi, it's for free I will take you wherever you want.'"

Actually, nearly half of the services in this city were for free; this was a bit weird but good as we didn't have witch city currency. We asked her to drop us at the best hotel. She agreed and we sat on the broomstick-taxi and went. After reaching the hotel, we felt as if the earth became upside down. We saw that everything was dirty in the room and there was a bad drainage type of smell. It was a literal prison; no one could take a breath there even for a minute.

Then George got an idea and he said, "Witches stink so the best room is made dirty but the worst room may be good and clean."

Tia exclaimed, "Good idea!"

Sid then asked the witch for the worst room in the worst hotel. She seemed confused and took us there. It was a mind-blowing luxurious room with a clean white bed and white walls. It was just amazing. I had never seen such a luxury in my life before. We decided to take some holiday enjoyment here for three days.

The first day we went to the worst witch restaurant and ate luxurious food; they served pizzas with cheese toppings and had all kinds of cheese such as mozzarella, chipotle and cheddar and they served yummy pancakes with a delicious touch of sweet maple syrup. Moving ahead to the second day, we went to the worst tourist attractions such as a space exploration centre where there were telescopes that could see into other planets. And there were statues of famous witch personalities. On the third and final day, we went to the worst swimming pool; nothing had been better than these three days of our quest. It was heartily enjoyable.

We then headed back to work. We examined the Witch City map, but we still couldn't find the psychic crystal. Finally, we asked a witch about the psychic crystal. She said, "Too gut da makiccustalyuhaaav too passs a tastthet no watch cud pas tl dat. If yuwunt too guet it go to da cenrallirary." (*To get the magic crystal you have to pass a test that no witch could pass till date, if you really want it, go to the central library.*)

We went ahead to the central library on the broomstick-taxi. When we reached there, we saw rows and rows of books on black magic and white magic and many secret potions and the history of witches. The stupidest witch was sitting there (*stupidest in Witch City means most intelligent*). The witch was an expert in the following studies.

Apology: study of Algae

Anthropology: study of Humans

Archaeology: study of Past human activity

Axiology: study of Values

Bacteriology: study of Bacteria

Biology: study of Life

Cardiology: study of Heart

Cosmology: study of Origin and laws of the universe

Cryptology: study of Codes

Cytology: study of Cells

Deontology: study of ethics

Enology: study of Wine

Entomology: study of Insects

Epidemiology: study of Disease

Epistemology: study of Knowledge

Eschatology: study of End of time

Ethnology: study of Animal behaviour

Etiology: study of Causation and origination

Geology: study of Earth

Gerontology: study of Aging

Hagiology: study of Saints

Herpetology: study of Amphibians and reptiles

Histology: study of Tissues of plants and animals

Horology: study of measuring time

Ichthyology: study of Fish

Kinesiology: study of Human movement

Limnology: study of Fresh inland water

Mammalogy: study of Mammals

Morphology: study of Form of organisms

Mycology: study of Fungi

Numismatology: study of Currency

Oncology: study of Tumors

Ontology: study of Reality

Ophthalmology: study of Eye

Ornithology: study of Birds

Palaeontology: study of Fossils

Pathology: study of Diseases

Philology: study of Language

Physiology: study of Functions of organisms

Psychology: study of mental functions and behaviours

Teleology: study of Final causes

Hematology: study of Dying and death

Virology: study of Viruses

Zoology: study of Animals

There are a lot more but I'm tired of reading for now!!

We were tired of reading the list of many degrees and graduation certificates she had. James was trying to estimate her backlogs. She was dressed in a good-looking suit. Jokes aside, I tried to speak to her. She spoke in a fine American accent and used twisting and turning words and complicated phrases just like a racing game where so many stunts are made to overtake opponents. We obviously took hours to talk using the Oxford Dictionary. We asked her about the psychic crystal. She gave us a weird stern look. She said to get the psychic crystal we must go on an adventure through the broken Trivia Game. We all started laughing and then Tina asked the witch, "Who can play a broken Game?" We burst out into laughter once again!! The witch got irritated. She gave us a look like how the teacher gives when we draw her face on the blackboard and bunk classes. She was a weightlifter too; she lifted me and my friends in her hand like an inflated balloon and took us to the broken game. The humour was that it wasn't a video game, it was an 18th century board game. We almost had created a world record of laughing consequently. Suddenly her face started to turn red. She swung us up in the air and threw us into the board game with extreme force.

Chapter 7

Into the Trivia Game

A Milky White portal took us in, and we fell onto the Trivia Game. Then Joe read the rules:

"Rules: -

-Choose only correct answers

-A wrong answer may cost you

We entered a tunnel, after reaching further there were five caves completely dark; we were confused but we still had a solution. I drew a pair of magical glasses with my magical paintbrush and then I could have a sneak peek through the caves, though it seemed as cheating but it doesn't really matter because we are saving the world. It was a type of glass that could see through things. George eagerly snatched it from me and looked through it; he saw three big giants and two small giants. We didn't understand this trivia game. I recalled the rules and tried figuring out this riddle. Tina started to show her MAS (Mental Aptitude Skills) now.

She said:-

"Small Giants = SG"

"Big Giants = BG"

"BG energy > SG energy"

"Therefore Trivia Game = Cave"

      Wrong answer = Big Giants

      Correct Answer = Small Giants

Anyways we didn't understand anything and slept like we were in a mathematics class when the teacher was giving a boring lecture.

Then she explained in proper English, "According to the rules TRIVIA GAME means the cave, SMALL GIANTS means correct answer because they are weaker than the big giants. BIG GIANTS are wrong answers because they are stronger. And it would be harder to defeat them."

We understood and went into the cave with the small giants with our magical guns in our hands. When we went in, we got stuck in the worst situation ever. As we entered the cave, the small giant was eating chicken. We went in slowly not knowing what to do. As soon as he saw us, he started crying and the three big giants came for no reason and were staring at us. I didn't even imagine this situation would occur. They had six fingers with nails of two inches or probably longer and rotten meat was stuck between their blackish-yellow teeth. Yuck! Their skin was green, and they were wearing clothes made of tiger skin, I was almost about to vomit. We then tried escaping the cave, but their fat bellies blocked us. Then James took the paintbrush from my backpack and drew a pepper spray and sprayed it in the giant's eyes. His drawing was not that good but anyways his idea worked. Even after the pepper spray, it was hard to escape through their giant bellies, but we made it! We went out and stepped into another cave where another small giant was relaxing; we sprayed pepper spray on him too. After exploring his cave, we found a golden door which was the exit of this trivia game, but however hard we tried we couldn't break through it.

The pepper spray effect on the big giants was about to finish soon, we were stuck in a nasty situation; suddenly, my unicorn friend came out of the fire crystal and gave a blockbuster entry. He kicked all the giants as if they were origami made by paper. Then his horn started shining like a magical diamond and a beam with a thickness of almost one-thousandth of a centimetre slowly moved towards the door as if it was going to reflect. We were completely puzzled about what our unicorn friend was trying to do. When the beam of light reached there a pin drop silence occurred, we were looking carefully and then BOOM!! The door blasted off and was broken into a fine powder and I realized a small spark can start a raging fire. I filled up a little powder in my bag. It was gold so it would definitely be worth millions of dollars.

Chapter 8

The Oceanic Miracle

We then escaped and found ourselves on a boat where I found the magic crystal and placed it in my bag. According to the map, the next water crystal was in the middle of the Malasobas Ocean. We were in the Oschabos Ocean and were moving ahead to the Malasobas Ocean. I checked the GPS, and we were at the same spot! It was like a horror movie. We boosted the engine faster and faster to move on the map. I spotted my ship moving slowly and slowly on the GPS but then I noticed that we were spinning round and round on the same spot. We tried boosting the engines as much as we could. Suddenly I noticed a small dot on the ocean and ignored it but as we went closer and closer to it I checked the latitudes and longitudes of the area, it was the ChaicoppaNali and that was the reason we were spinning round and round at the same point!! The ChaicoppaNali is the deepest point in this magical world; it has strong ocean currents and waves which forms a force that spins and then pulls us inside. We were trying our best, but we struggled a lot and even our unicorn friend tried to help us. But we failed. Then I got a fantastic idea. I told everyone to draw a few boosters with my paintbrush. Our ship was continuously moving closer and closer to the ChaicoppaNali and the currents got stronger and stronger. After we drew the boosters and made them ready, we all attached the boosters to the boat with a rope and tried moving forward. Then the ship was increasing its acceleration and speed and we were moving away from the ChaicoppaNali. We thought we were saved but another worst event added insult to injury. A large fish, the size of a teenage whale, pounced on us OMG!! It was a megalodon.

Fact File: -

Megalodon, meaning "big tooth", is an extinct species of shark that lived approximately 23 to 3.6 million years ago, during the Early Miocene to the Pliocene epoch. It was formerly thought to be a close relative of the great white shark.

They were extinct but I don't know how it came there and then suddenly the large ship started breaking due to the ocean currents formed by the megalodon's movements and then the huge megalodon bashed on us and it pained as if the earth had been separated into half. And we all got separated from each other. After we woke up, we found ourselves in an unknown place. I checked the latitudes and found that we were in the Malasobas Ocean. I was surprised, we were underwater, and we could breathe easily. We didn't know who brought us here. The only thing we decided then was that as we were in the Malasobas Ocean we were to search for the crystal of water. None of us could believe that we were at the ocean bed and could walk upright and easily breathe. I call this the Oceanic Miracle; it was just miraculous. Sid was slapping, pinching and hurting himself trying to prove that this was a dream, but it was not. As we moved forward, we found many varieties and diversity of fishes and suddenly we noticed a human face; we all were shocked when we went forward to see what that was...

Chapter 9

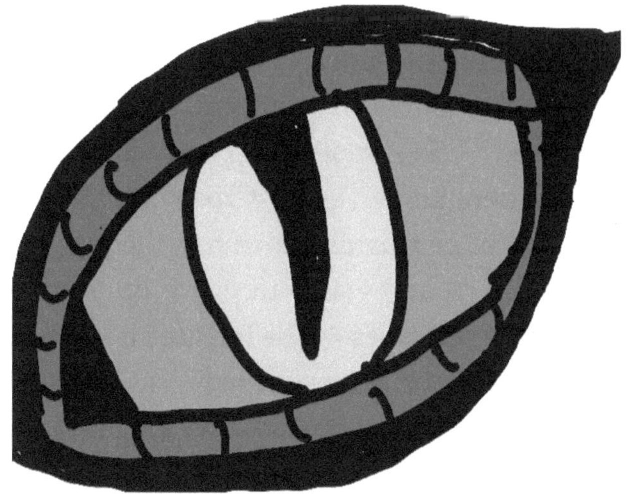

Mr Crocodile

And to my surprise, it was a mermaid. Sid and James fainted. We had never seen one in real life. She came towards us and said, "Welcome to the Atlantic City." I never knew mermaids could speak English. Though her English was not perfect, it was somewhat better than the English which the broomstick-taxi driver in the witch land spoke. I named her English Merminlish.

We followed her and went to the queen of mermaids. She looked dull and sad. I thanked her for calling us here and then I asked, "What happened mermaid queen, you look unpleased?" She replied, "There is a mad scientist here known as Mr Crocodile. He stole the wand of mermaids which had the precious magical stone and wants to prove himself the Lord of the seven seas. If he misuses it, Atlantic City would be transformed to an ugly graveyard. And now he thinks we are his slaves and threatens us by black mailing to destroy the Atlantic City."

We started discussing this amongst ourselves, but at the drop of a hat, George agreed to defeat the crocodile. We had no option left, so we said OKAY to the mermaid queen and then continued. The mermaid Queen told us that Mr Crocodile lives in the darkest area of the Atlantic Ocean facing northwest. After the little conversation with the queen, we asked George why he accepted to defeat Mr Crocodile, and he gave the world's stupidest reason. He said, "In my sister's fairy tale book I read a page that if you do a favour to the mermaid, they give you a delicious feast and mermaids are brilliant chefs." I gave him a tight slap and then we moved ahead rapidly to the northwest as the mermaid queen said, until we saw a small undersea volcano. To be safe we used the special pair of goggles which we used in the trivia game to see through things. This volcano was fake; it was the science lab of the mad scientist Mr Crocodile; he was standing on two legs just like humans did and was wearing a white coat like a scientist. The funniest thing was that he was not a crocodile. He was an alligator and we all started laughing out loud. The only visible difference between a crocodile and an alligator is that crocodiles have longer and pointed snouts while alligators have shorter and more rounded snouts. His teeth looked sharp and dangerous. Instead of attacking at first, we went into a small cave near that fake volcano and started discussing what plan we should execute.

He was a mad scientist, and he may have many potions and secret spells so we couldn't compete with him easily. We created a plan: all seven of us would enter from different directions and surround him. We entered the fake volcano from different sides, Sid and

James who were near the two power plants damaged them and there was no light or any electricity. Tina was near the garage, where she took out parts of his submarine. I was near the chemical lab where the alligator was, it was a critical place. I disabled all his scientific gadgets by replacing their batteries. I inserted a special battery in them with a computer virus; if he would enable them, they would explode like little dynamites. I was an expert in making computer viruses with C++. I threw all his chemical substances on the floor. He had nothing left then except his magical wand which was in his hand. He was sitting on a chair in the middle of the lab. We all entered the lab and were hiding. I gave everyone a signal and then we started attacking. He could teleport! He had a teleporting device that helped him go here and there and attacks were almost of no use. He was teleporting at a constant speed and only at a few fixed places and always came behind us and started throwing seashells it hurts! We all went near the walls of the lab. I spoke to everyone on the walkie talkie and said, "Maybe there is a checkpoint he uses to teleport." There were small green balls that blinked when he teleported. I shot all of them with my laser Dragunov. He then tried operating the teleporting machine but was unsuccessful. We bound him in ropes with the grappling hook gun and took the magic wand from his hands, and then I noticed that the magic wand had the water crystal. George gave me a wicked stare and then gave me a tight slap in return for what I had done before.

Finally, we brought him in front of the queen. She looked pleased. She questioned us about the crystal. We told her the reason we needed it for, and she said Okay. We were satisfied too. The mermaid queen offered us a feast that night and gave us food to use in our long journey. As George had said, they were great chefs. George once again stared at me and gave me another tight slap and said, "One slap for slapping me without any reason and another slap for eating this delicious food made by the mermaids". I was angry but didn't do anything. It was my mistake. If we had declined the mermaid queen's request, we couldn't have found the magic crystal. We moved to the next destination…

Chapter 10

In The jungle

And the next destination was the Dangaus Jungle where we would find the crystal of nature. I hated the place. It was filled with varieties and diversities of reptiles, those creepy little creatures who crawl upon us. Yuck! We were tired out, so we didn't want to meet anyone such as a panther, tiger or creepy-crawly spider and other reptiles' etcetera. This was a jungle so some weird plants might also be dangerous. So, we first decided to rest under a tree which was pretty weirdly shaped after all this was a weird place. After a few minutes we continued and we moved further and further and finally, we found a huge Peepal tree and on its branch, was the crystal of nature. I thought we could easily pick this up and return but it was not that easy.

We climbed the tree and picked the crystal up and were happily returning when a giant orangutan like creature came and grabbed us. He was followed by a group of them and one of them snatched the crystal. They were playing football with us and throwing us up and down and kicking us.

Finally, after everyone was tired one orangutan gave all of them a signal and they tied us with ropes and brought us to some unknown den The Orangutan Palace.

He asked us, "Why are you here?" His English was a bit different, so I named it Oranglish. These people were too weird. First of all, I didn't understand what he thought of us as, friends or foes.

Chapter 11

The Orangutanic Disco Laws

Without more conversation, he switched on the disco lights and then we all started dancing with tender coconuts in our hands. I didn't know orangutans had disco lights too. The music was very weird. It was a six-word lyric "ku-koo-ka-kaa-ki-kee". I didn't know how to dance so I just followed the orangutans. I named this the Orangutanic disco.

After five minutes the orangutan king stopped the disco and asked the same question, "Why are you here?"

There were thirty seconds of deathly silence and then Tina was about to say something, but the orangutan king again started the disco and the same thing happened. I got angry and politely said, "Give us a chance to speak!" and everything stopped.

Then a judge came inside the hall, and he opened a fat book and said, "According to law number 54,747,064,145,686 (fifty-four trillion seven hundred forty seven billion sixty four million one hundred and forty five thousand six hundred sixty eight) disturbing Orangutans while disco is a serious crime. The creature that goes against this law will be jailed for 3 years."

The Orangutans said kaw-kaw-kee-kee and pushed us into a cage. I didn't say anything wrong, and what a bunch of infinite stupid laws do they have.

Now we had only one option: we had to do a melee fight with orangutans. James and Tina started to create a device with my magical paintbrush. They were experts in mechanics. After hours they created their new invention, the orangutan palms. While wearing these gloves we would have the powers to climb on walls and do Kungfu like orangutans. We could also do dance-fighting with this. We first bent the iron rods of the cage and then we escaped. The orangutan king seemed shocked to see us.

Sid exclaimed, "Turn on the disco!!"

One of the orangutans did so and we started dance-fighting like professionals. Our hands and legs were moving on by themselves thanks to the orangutan palm device. We tied up the king in a jiffy too and then we grabbed the crystal of nature and escaped the jungle. I had never felt so strong. So now we had four out of seven of these crystals. We then moved on to the next destination…

Chapter 12

Animal Gadgets

Okay, so the next destination was the city of black clouds where we would find the crystal of Thunder. I wondered how to go there. I thought we would need some kind of aircraft or a space jet, but James and Tina were only two people in our team who knew mechanical engineering, so if they worked now, it would take them a month or two to complete it.

Then Tia snatched my bag and removed the fire crystal and called "Hey Pega-corn we need your help!" Oh! How didn't I get this idea. Everyone sighed.

We all excitedly sat on the Pega-corn and said, "LET'S GO!!!" but the Pega-corn fell down. It said, "I'm too hungry for now, is there any food?" We were feeling hungry too.

We opened our tiffins which the mermaids had given to us. All the tiffin boxes were empty except mine because it was password protected. I thought some animal would steal it in the jungle, so I had locked it. Then George whispered, "Actually friends in the orangutan prison I was feeling very hungry so I…" before he completed the sentence everyone, including the Pega-corn, gave him a death stare and then we all gave him a tight slap on his face.

Then Sid got an idea and he asked, "James and Tina can you make other animal parts such as the orangutan gloves, elephants' trunk, bear claws and eagles wings, monkeys limbs?" I forgot to mention but Sid was an expert in zoology (study of animals). James replied, "But what is the use of them??" Sid said, "Elephant's trunk can help us create a small house from tree trunks, bear claws can help us catch fish from the lake, eagle wings would help us spot food from heights easily, and we can prepare food on our own."

We all were with Sid. We helped Tina and James in creating the devices. After a couple of hours, the gadgets were ready. We all distributed our work. Tia was the eagle co-operating with me and Sid who were the monkeys. She spotted fruits while flying and we climbed the trees to collect them. And on the other hand, Tina and James were the bears picking up fish from the lake. George was the elephant who was building the campfire and a small house because there was scorching heat. We all worked together. Pega-corn was too tired, so he was resting under the shade of a tree. After all the work was done, we moved ahead to cook. I had never dared to fry a fish. Once while frying the fish, I kept it on high flame and the fish became ashes. Tia knew the fish fry recipe which her grandma told her she instructed, and everybody was making fish fry except me. I was making fruit juice, salad and tender coconut juice. Everyone fried their own fish except me; Tia made one fish fry for me. Then after a few minutes, our food was ready.

The fish fry that Tia made was enjoyable, George fried it too much, James added too much spice, Sid's fish was half raw and half fried poor him, Tina's fish was kind of good. I had thought we would make five-star food, but this was zero-star food or you can also call it starless food. After the starless fish, everyone drank my fruit juice. It was really very nice. At least now I got some summer enjoyment. After this, we gave some food to the Pega-corn and then we moved ahead into the clouds…

Chapter 13

The clouded arena

Our Pega-corn friend took us into the clouds where we needed an oxygen mask, so we used the ones which we made in the land of volcanoes. We were 15,000 feet above sea level. And I really didn't understand how we were able to walk on the clouds. This place was packed with dense clouds; hence I call it the clouded arena. I noted all these special names made by me in a small pocket diary so that I could tell the experience to my teacher and my parents. Then I spotted a small glass box in which I could see something shining brightly. I went a bit forward and then I saw that it was the crystal of thunder. I didn't want to fall into a trap again like in the jungle with the orangutans. So I searched the whole area using a thermal cam but I could see nothing so I moved forward with my friends slowly and slowly. Then I thought there is nothing to fear so I went and opened the glass case, picked up the crystal and went back but suddenly out of nowhere a strong muscular arm came out and pulled us into the crystal case. We all fell down and down and landed in some unknown place.

Then I saw a throne and the darkness started disappearing a bit and I could see a person sitting on it! He looked like a cartoon superhero, but I think he was another silly supervillain who trapped us while we were trying to get the crystal.

Oh! Come on! I didn't want to face another villain. He had a lightning hammer in his hand and a grey beard. I wondered where his walking stick was as he looked like a ninety-year-old person probably he used his hammer as a walking stick. His muscles were cool looking, just like the ones which I wanted to have. Now all the darkness was gone. We both could see each other's faces. But his eyes were closed! He was literally sleeping. And now he started drooling. OMG! Why was he sleeping? Then we slowly tried escaping from there but the worst thing was that as we were trying to escape lightning struck.

Chapter 14

The King of Thunder

That old fellow woke up. I tried to negotiate with him for the crystal, "Hi I am Ratan. Happy to meet you." But I don't think he was happy to meet us. In reply, he threw a knife towards me but thank God I dodged it.

This person looked dangerous and then suddenly he stood up and started throwing current waves on us. Because of our specialized soldier suit, we were able to face it but then he threw a special cage and we got locked in it. Oh God, another prison!!

We then created a plan. George told us electricity spreads by water and is stopped by rubber. After creating a plan, we started executing it. I knew how to pick locks, but the lock was electrically charged so I wore rubber gloves and picked the lock. Then we slowly escaped but unfortunately, his sharp eyes noticed us so then we moved to plan B.

I was holding a water bottle and George lifted me with the elephant gadget. He swung me up in the air and threw me towards that king with extreme force. The king was shooting at me with his hammer, but he failed and then when I reached above his head, I opened the bottle and spilt water on his hammer and him and luckily the plan worked. You might be wondering what the plan was; let me explain, when he shot volts of electricity the water on the hammer conducted it to his body and you might know that the human body is a good conductor of electricity and hence, he burnt off with his own shock. We took the thunder crystal and escaped that place. Now we had Five of those crystals and only two were left.

The next destination was the central library and we had to find the crystal of knowledge.

Chapter 15

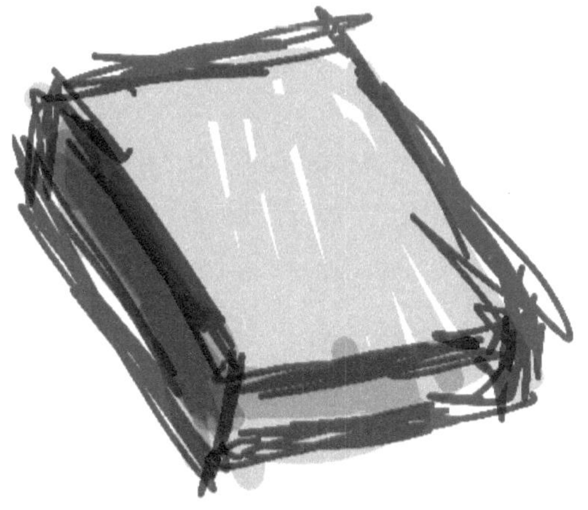

Reading Break!!

Finally, we reached the talking library. The library was more like a country; it was humongous with over a hundred floors. I hoped there wouldn't be any problem here because my pocket diary had only seven pages left. Ok jokes aside, we walked into the library and there were tons of books. In fact, we all loved reading interesting books, so we halted our quest here and took some time in reading our favourite books. Tia was spending her time on cookbooks and fashion magazines; Tina was reading about traditional dances and music. James was reading a guide about mechanical engineering. George was reading how to enjoy delicious food, what a stupid book wonder who the author was! Sid was reading an encyclopedia about wildlife. I rather spent my time on some cat videos on youtube.

After a couple of hours, we got back to work. The library was huge, and we didn't know where the crystal would be. hours passed and we covered the whole library, but we still didn't find the crystal.

Then I tripped and my hand pulled a book out. Suddenly from nowhere a thud sound came and the bookshelf flipped and there was the crystal. I grabbed it but an old lady came and knocked us into a pile of books, huh I am done with this. She said, "Do this homework if you want the crystal."

I said "WHAT????"

See pls listen you old lady we are saving the earth and you should be proud of us I don't know what silly problem you guys have with us taking the crystal and it was more than a hundred books and then from my bag, the statue soul woke up and said he will do all the homework we were pleased. All the homework was about the bronze age and its language then in a second the statue soul had completed all the homework with magic but we are saving the world so cheating isn't a problem and we were let go with the crystal. This place was easy, all thanks to the statue soul who did the magic(cheating). We then moved ahead to the next destination for the last crystal.

Chapter 16

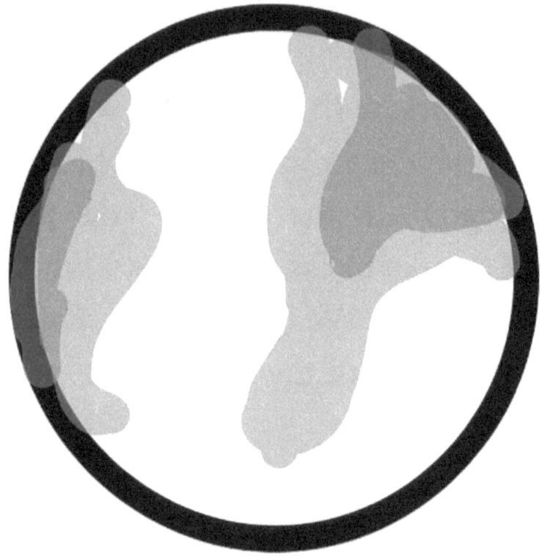

Outer Space

The next destination was outer space! "WHAT??" said James. We were completely exhausted. Then everyone tried to think of an idea.

"Let's call our Pega-corn friend," said George. We called the Pega-corn, but he said, "I can only fly by pushing air down by my wings but there is no air in outer space." He went back in the fire crystal. Then I got an idea. We could use our superbikes. Everyone agreed! There was an option called space jet mode, we activated it and the bikes transformed into small capsule-like rockets. We made sure everything was packed. We then sat in it and read the manual and controls. And then we were all set to go.

We went up to space. It was a little hard, our heads were spinning and ears popped due to the atmospheric pressure but we made it and we were out of the gravitational field. Then I exactly had no idea where we would find the crystal of heavenly bodies in this large outer space. And then BOOM! An asteroid crashed into James, and he was being pulled towards a black hole! We followed him and we went to the black hole but unfortunately, we were pulled inside too.

There was nothing except darkness and a shining star. I thought that the star was also trapped in the black hole. The black hole was pulling some junk inside and was hurting us. A piece of space junk pushed me deeper, and I went near the star and then I found it to be the crystal of planets. Everyone cheered but we were still stuck in the black hole so what could we do. Then Sid gave another idea from his encyclopedia, he said, "The black hole has an exit that leads us to the white hole." So we tried finding the exit. There was nothing except darkness there. Then I got pulled by something else. James said that's the exit and everyone came with me. The white hole then threw us with force on mars as if it was vomiting. We fled to mars. I thought we would fall down and bump our heads, but our spacesuits were strong enough.

Chapter 17

Hidden secrets

Tia questioned, "We have all the crystals, what now?"

The statue soul then jumped out of my bag and asked to hand over the crystals to him. I went near him and instead of giving him the crystals, BASH! I broke the statue! Then I returned to my friends and told them the actual story.

FLASHBACK: - All the stories that the statue soul was blabbering were just fake. Let me tell the real story. First of all, Mighty Ranges wasn't a king, he was an evil person who wanted to defeat the gods. And that rock was just a toy, let me explain how. When I fell down the cliff in the land of volcanoes, I had fainted as you all remember, and time had literally stopped! My soul had exited the body, and I could see the heavens in afterlife. I heard a voice which told me the actual story. And one of the biggest secrets was that the statue soul was Mighty Ranges himself. I didn't destroy the statue nor tell these secrets to you before because we needed the statue soul's help to find the crystals. He was the one who did the oceanic miracle, and we were able to breathe and walk upright at the ocean bed without getting crushed by the pressure down there. He was the one who made us able to walk on clouds. He was the one who gave us this armour, suit and our superbikes. He was the one who did the homework in the library.

After the flashback, everyone knew the real story and then the statue soul was separated from the statue and became an individual soul. Everyone feared it but I knew how to solve the problem in a jiffy.

I said the golden spell that the voice in the heaven had given to me, "Esko-sisco-zum,azony-zumzum. *(The evil should be finished, let's unite and finish him.)*" Then all the crystals and the Pega-corn and my friends started to merge in one form, and we applied extreme power and then he was killed forever, and everything was over…

Chapter 18

Happy Ending

Then I found myself on my bed, and my parents and Wolfy were there too. The next day, I talked to my friends and surprisingly they didn't remember anything and unluckily it was the last day of my vacation. I missed my ice cream and the beach, but I was proud of myself that I saved the world.

Then the next day, my school bus didn't come. I wandered around and then went back home and I received a email on my mom's phone, and it said that the school had extended holidays for two more weeks. I was pretty sure god had given this to me as a thank you gift! I then told my parents about my adventure, but they didn't believe it and said it's just a nightmare. I also thought so because my friends didn't remember the adventure. But while bathing I noticed two scars on my left leg. That was the only proof I had about my adventure. Then my father encouraged me to write a book on this adventure. I wasn't a good writer, but I tried my best. I published it and was only waiting for readers' responses. After two weeks I noticed that my book was good, and I got emails asking for my next book. And then after publishing it, the next month in the daily newspaper the first headline was about my book. It said that "The Book That Became A Bestseller In A Week's time!" My book had one people's hearts I was pleased, and everyone was proud of me. Would you like to read it? And the good news is that you've just finished reading it…

About The Author

Hi, I am Ratan Vinnu, from, India, the author and illustrator of this book. I am the youngest novella writer and book illustrator. I am an Author, Amateur Film Maker, Animator, Computer Graphics Artist, Sound Designer, Game Developer, Coder and YouTuber. Follow me on my social media.

https://www.tumblr.com/blog/ratanvinnuproductions

https://www.instagram.com/ratan_vinnu/

https://www.facebook.com/ratan.vinnu/

https://www.artstation.com/vinnu_cg

https://imgur.com/user/RatanVinnu/posts

https://www.youtube.com/channel/UC6QkQmLa80aQ9S3QFJxOckw

GiveAway

Top 50 Ways to Say Hello In Different Languages

Hi friends so this is my giveaway section. In every book there's one for sure. In my giveaway section, I share a piece of knowledge that you can use in your daily life. So, in this book, I have shared 50 ways of saying hello. You can impress your friends and relatives with these 50 hellos.

1. Afrikaans: Hallo

2. Albanian: Përshëndetj (*PershenDEATye*)

3. Arabic: مرحبا (*marhabaan*)

4. Azerbaijani: Salam

5. Basque: Kaixo

6. Breton: Demat

7. Bulgarian: Здравейте (*Zdraveĭte*)

8. Catalan: Hola

9. Chichewa: Moni

10. Corsican: Bonghjornu

11. Croatian: Bok

12. Czech: Ahoj

13. Danish: Hej

14. Dutch: Hallo

15. English: Hello

16. Esperanto: Saluton

17. Estonian: Tere

18. Filipino: Kamusta

19. Finnish: Hei

20. French: Bonjour

21. Georgian: მიესალმები (*miesalmebi*)

22. German: Hallo

23. Greek: Χαίρε (*chai-ray*)

24. Hausa: Hello

25. Hebrew: שלום (*shalom*)

26. Hindi: नमस्ते (*namaste*)

27. Hungarian: Helló

28. Irish: Diadhuit

29. Korean: 안녕하세요 (*yuobosevo*)

30. Italian: Ciao

31. Lao: ສະບາຍດີ (*sabaidi*)

32. Latin: Salve

33. Lithuanian: Sveiki

34. Maltese: Bongu

35. Nepali: नमस्ते (*namaste*)

36. Pashto: سلام (*salam*)

37. Portugese: Olá

38. Romanian: Buna

39. Samoan: Talofa

40. Shona: Mhoro

41. Slovak: Ahoj

42. Slovenian: Zdravo

43. Spanish: Hola

44. Swahili: Hodi

45. Tamil: வணக்கம் (*vanakaam*)

46. Turkish: Merhaba

47. Vietnamese: chàobạn

48. Welsh: Helo

49. Yiddish: העלא (*hela*)

50. Zulu: Sawubon